Title: A visual hug
© 2019, Andrés J. Colmenares
www.wawawiwacomics.com

Printed by Amazon

ISBN: 9798657483895

 @wawawiwacomics

 /wawawiwacomics

To our dear followers and online friends, for all the support we've received to bring this book to life. You are the best! And a special visual hug with extra chocolate syrup to our beloved **'TOP 150 FANS'**, you guys were the first group to purchase this special book.

★ TOP 150 FANS ★

Valérie Minelli · Eszter Szücs-Mátyás · Sohan Rao · Lisa Beaudet · Amber Diana · Zeiter Florian · Robert Pascal Bakker · Michelle Sager · David Yoo · Oda Garvik · Jake Mclean · Candice Quadros · Ziggy Chicano · Tommi Kaisto · Ravenslark Yap CS · Patricia Sørlie · Sahand Fard · Saurab Saha · Gabi Stoffan · Riso Stoffan · Victor Sutherland · Coralie Raffort · Sabine Astier · Isabel Hou · Hugo · Beatriz Hernández · Christian Mueller · Arica Lewis · Nora Al-Nasser · Tahani Al-Omran · Thomas Oberhammer · Jossy Zamora · Catherine Soesile · Gabe · Jason W. Borges · Felicia Tam · Olga Kuroyedova · Savannah · Kayla Brown · Crumpet Goober · Guy Kopsombut · Anja Raabe · Lincy Rachel George · Nicolas Le Drézen · Jeffries · Dustin Schuchholz · Friede Kumpe · Salena Su · Veera Siva Sri Aditya Katam · Parnian Farnam · Tyler Uttech · SuperWoody64 · Kaitlyn Twombly · Amalie Solvberg · André Almeida · Lucy Li · Martin Pfannee · Maik Niendorf · Edoardo de gaetano · Eileen Weber · BEE PHAM · caroflamingo · Cappy Kwong · Calum Ridell · Julia Grundmann · Bethany Tan · Livia Rocha · Maria Padilla · Joshua Rewerts · YogiJo · Dawn Goodger · blamethewolf · Michaela Hall · Joedoe · Michael Jan · Daniel Rogers · Emilyn Chee · Malika Jean Louis · Selene Verhofstad · JZ · Sophy Gao · Jocelyne Salinas · FLOFLOFLY · Samantha Barth · Michelle Kim · Cristina Le · Alex Lew · Elba Elizabeth Velasco · Vera O'Herne-Visser · Carole Genoud · Robert J. Holcomb III · Lakshmi Upadhyaya Kalmanje · Nina Setyaningsih · Ankur · Linda Sabrina · Gloria Cota · Annie Samis · Emily Van Bergen · Eunice Tong · Julia · Tom Corke · Marta Medio Menendez · Romain Nienajadlo · Jamie Chung · Hugues Rieublandou · Ashlen LeClaire · Melanie Bois · Ursina Baitella · Thao Ly · Torsten Koplin · Yannick Unterlauf · Zacchaeus Yeo · Navina ·

★ TOP 150 FANS ★

Bailey Lewis · Jeanette Wu =^._.^= · Amanda Pagul · Anousone Kitisa · Joyce Lee · Mark Sashegyi · Laurajane Sutter · Myint Myat Hein · Jessica Fournier · Ashley Hardwick · Grace Méridan · Sow Ayad · Fatin Nuwairah · Fabian Benninghoven · Alexa Polizos · Brandon Mendonsa · Nydia Cavazos · Isabel Taylor · MAGDA · Stacey Lyons · Judith Nieto · Prakriti Akash · Reinhard Hafenscher · Mégane Ecoffard · Vicki Strahan · Amit Panda · Quyen Ta · Emeline Langlois · Mohit Sharma · Ádám Szücs-Mátyás.

We really hope you love this book, everyone!

- Andrés J. Colmenares & Viviana Navas.

THANKS!

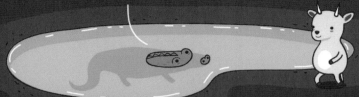

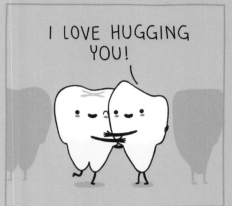
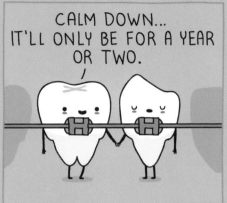
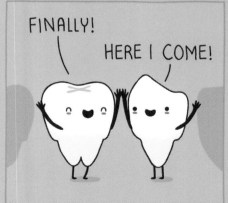
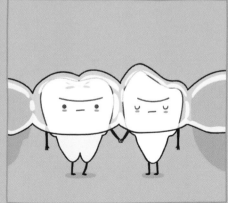

THE INTERRUPTER

I BROKE IT, HOW CAN I PAY YOU?

DO I SIT IN FRONT OR NEXT TO HER?

JUST WING IT, YOU WON'T MAKE HER FEEL UNCOMFORTABLE.

ME IN MY PROFILE PIC.

ME IN REAL LIFE.

IRRITABLE BOWEL

OPTION A

YOU CAN'T FLY.

YOU CAN'T FLY.

OPTION B

YOU CAN FLY.

YOU CAN FLY.

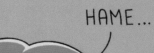

STEPS TO ATTRACT SOMEONE:

APPROACH WITH CONFIDENCE.

BREAK THE ICE.

⌁SUCCESS⌁

THAT'S
ENOUGH!

WE ARE GATHERED
HERE TODAY
TO JOIN THESE TWO...

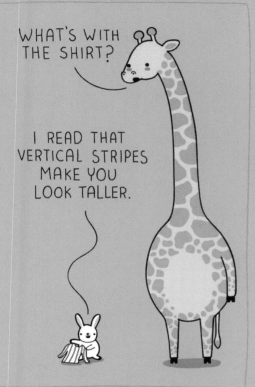
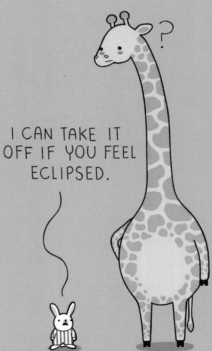

BINGE WATCHING

BEFORE YOUR 20s

AFTER

CAN I JOIN YOU?

YOU'VE GOT THINGS TO DO.

GUILT

YOU ARE SO SILLY.

I GOT PAID!

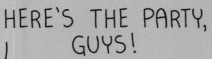

HERE'S THE PARTY, GUYS!

PARANORMAL ACTIVITIES

TURN INTO RAISINS TOGETHER

PEOPLE AT THE BEACH.

ME.

LIFE CYCLE OF PASTA

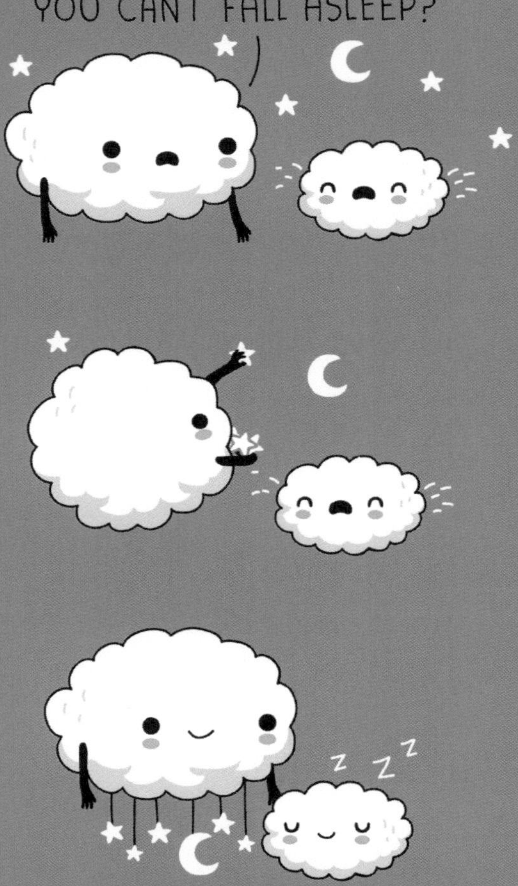
YOU CAN'T FALL ASLEEP?
Z Z Z

WELL, I'M STUCK IN BED.

IT'S ONLY A DATE,
JUST DON'T FALL IN LOVE.

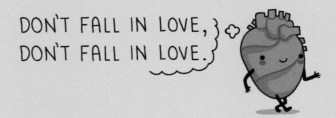

SMILES ARE CONTAGIOUS

LET'S PLAY!

GOD, WHY DID
YOU TAKE HIM?!

I'M DOING
YOGA.

PEOPLE DRINKING WATER

ME

DON'T CONFORM IN LIFE, TRY TO REACH FOR THE STARS.

DONE! NOW WHAT?

WELL, WELL,
LOOK WHO'S BACK AND
BROUGHT A LITTLE
FRIEND!

THEY WERE THE
ONES BULLYING
ME.

THANKS.

OK, IT IS SCARY, I WON'T DO IT AGAIN.

YOU FELL FROM HEAVEN.

MONDAY

TUESDAY

WEDNESDAY

THURSDAY

FRIDAY

OTHER PEOPLE IN THE GYM

ME

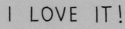

TRUE LOVE

STORIES

NEVER

END

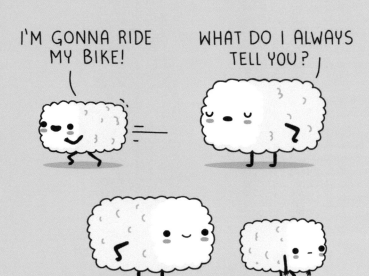

LOOK HOW FAR WE'VE COME.

SEE? MY MOM HAS
THE BIGGEST
HEART IN THE WORLD.

IT'S COMING OUT THROUGH HER HEAD.

WHOA.

WHY ARE YOU ALWAYS DOING THAT?

I'M TRAINING.

FOR WHAT?

THIS.

AH, A FANTASTIC SUMMER DAY.

OK, NO.

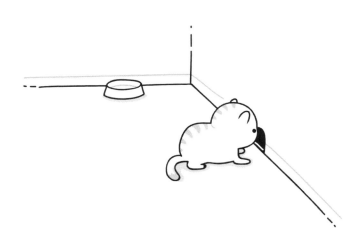

I LOVE YOU
THIS MUCH.

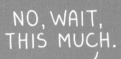

NO, WAIT,
THIS MUCH.

I DON'T THINK I CAN CATCH YOU BY MYSELF.

LET ME GET SOME HELP.

LET'S DO THIS.

WHAT'S WRONG
WITH YOUR SHELL?

I'M GOING CAMPING.

NOT HOT ENOUGH. NOT HOT ENOUGH.

NOT HOT ENOUGH. PERFECT.

SO WEAK AND VULNERABLE.

LET'S PUT AN END TO HIS MISERY.

DO WHAT YOU LOVE.

NOTICE THE GOOD.

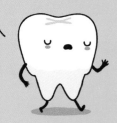

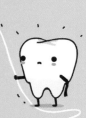

Printed in Great Britain
by Amazon

20358697R00080